Sebastian's Promise

written by Gwen Molnar

illustrated by Kendra McCleskey

A Hodgepog Book

Hodgepog Books and The Books Collective acknowledge the ongoing support of the Canada Council for the Arts and the Alberta Foundation for the Arts for our publishing program. We also acknowledge the support of the City of Edmonton and the Edmonton Arts Council

Editors for Press:
Mary Woodbury, Glen Huser

Cover design by Robert Woodbury
Inside layout by Dianne J. Cooper at The Books Collective
in Century Schoolbook, Arial, Times New Roman, Arial Black
and Palatino   (True-Type Font)
in Windows Quark X-Press 4.0.
Printed at Hignell Press

A Hodgepog Book for Kids

Published in Canada by Hodgepog Books, a member of:
The Books Collective,
214-21 10405 Jasper Avenue,
Edmonton, Alberta, T5J 3S2.
Telephone (780) 448 0590

Canadian Cataloguing in Publishing Data
Molnar, Gwen
Sebastian's Promise

ISBN 1895836-65-4

I.McCleskey,Kendra, 1965- II. Title
PS8576.O4515S42 1999   jC813'.54   C99-910699-6
PZ7.H73515Se 1999

Dedicated to

Doris Robbins

with gratitude

for your sustained interest

and support

1. Sebastian Has a Secret

Sebastian sat up in bed. His room was very dark. He could hear the wind whispering through the pine trees outside his window.

He could feel the wind blowing into his room. His room was very, very cold.

1

"Why is my window open so wide?" he wondered. Then he remembered. Last night Mom said, "It's so warm out tonight, I'm going to leave your window wide open, Sebastian."

It was not warm now. Sebastian got out of bed and went to close his window. He felt his bare feet getting cold and wet.

"Why are my feet getting cold and wet?" Sebastian wondered. Something cold and wet blew against his face. "It's snow!" said Sebastian. "Snow everywhere!"

Sebastian closed his window and looked out into the night.

Snow covered the hedge.

Snow covered the flowers.

Snow covered the sidewalk.

Snow covered the driveway.

The snow was falling in big huge snowflakes.

It looked deep and very beautiful.

"Wow!" whispered Sebastian. Sebastian dashed back to bed and got under the covers. He rubbed his cold feet until they felt warm.

"Nobody but me knows about this snow storm," thought Sebastian. "It's my secret until morning."

Sebastian began to go back to sleep. He was thinking about how wonderful the world looked covered with deep, white snow.

2. Sebastian Hears a Howl

Sebastian was almost asleep when he heard a strange sound.

"That can't be the wind," said Sebastian, "I closed the window tight."

4

Sebastian heard the sound again.

"Somebody is crying," said Sebastian.

Sebastian went to the door of his room and opened it.

Sebastian listened. He heard the cry again.

Sebastian went to Nana's door and listened. Nana was not crying.

Sebastian went to Mom and Dad's door and listened. Mom and Dad were not crying.

Sebastian went to Jennifer's door and listened. Jennifer was crying.

Sebastian opened Jennifer's door. Jennifer's room was very, very cold.

Sebastian turned on Jennifer's light. He saw Jennifer sitting on the side of her bed.

He saw Jennifer's wide open window. He saw snow blowing in Jennifer's window.

Sebastian closed Jennifer's window.

"Are you cold?" asked Sebastian.

"Yes," cried Jennifer.

"Is that why you're crying?" asked Sebastian.

"No," cried Jennifer.

"Then, why are you crying?" asked Sebastian.

"I'm crying because my ear is hurting and hurting," cried Jennifer, " and I'm crying because I can't find my Doolie Lamb."

Sebastian looked at Jennifer's ear. It was all red and swollen.

"I'll get Mom and Dad," said Sebastian. Sebastian ran to Mom and Dad's room and banged on the door.

"Come quick!" yelled Sebastian. "Jennifer's ear is hurting and hurting."

Mom hurried out. She was putting on her robe.

Dad hurried out. He was putting on his slippers.

Nana hurried out.

"What is going on?" asked Nana.

"Jennifer's ear is hurting and hurting," said Sebastian, "and she can't find her Doolie Lamb."

Mom and Dad and Nana and Sebastian all ran into Jennifer's room.

❉ ❉ ❉ ❉ ❉

3. Sebastian Gets the Blame

"I'll hold Jennifer," said Dad.

"I'll call the doctor," said Mom.

"I'll look for Doolie Lamb," said Sebastian.

"I'll make cocoa," said Nana.

Sebastian looked under Jennifer's blankets. Doolie Lamb was not there.

Sebastian looked under Jennifer's bed. Doolie Lamb was not there.

Sebastian looked in Jennifer's toy box. Doolie Lamb was not there.

"I cannot find Doolie Lamb," said Sebastian.

"You had Doolie Lamb," cried Jennifer. "We were playing hide the lamb before supper."

"Yes, I did have Doolie," said Sebastian, "But I'm sure I gave him back to you."

"No you didn't! No you didn't, 'Bastian!" cried Jennifer. "My Doolie Lamb's lost and it's all your fault!"

"Oh dear," said Mom. "Doctor Miller says we must take Jennifer to the hospital right away."

"The snow is very deep outside," said Sebastian. "The car might get stuck in the driveway."

"I'll get dressed and shovel the driveway so we can get the car out," said Dad.

"I'll get dressed and help you shovel the driveway," said Sebastian.

"I'll get dressed and wrap up Jennifer," said Mom.

"I'll hold Jennifer while you all get dressed," said Nana.

"I WANT MY DOOLIE LAMB," yelled Jennifer. "It's all your fault, 'Bastian!'"

"I'll find your lamb, Jennifer, I promise I will," said Sebastian. "But first I have to help Dad shovel the driveway."

4. Sebastian Ploughs a Path

"The snow is very deep," said Dad. He dug a wide path with his wide shovel.

"The snow is very, very deep," said Sebastian. He tried to dig a narrow path with his narrow shovel. It was very hard work.

Dad said, "You can keep the path I make free from new snow."

Sebastian pushed the new snow out of the way.

Back and forth, back and forth went Sebastian as he pushed away the new snow.

"That's as good as we can do," said Dad. "I'll go and get Mom and Jennifer."

"I'll keep all the new snow off the path," said Sebastian.

Back and forth, back and forth went Sebastian as he pushed away the new snow.

The big garage door opened. Sebastian saw Dad open the car door for Mom. She was carrying Jennifer in a big blue blanket.

Jennifer was crying and crying,
"I want my Doolie Lamb!"

"Sebastian will find it for you," said Mom.

"Run in the house now, Sebastian," said Dad.

"You've done a fine job of pushing the new snow away. Thank you."

"You're welcome," said Sebastian.

Sebastian and Nana stood in the doorway. They watched the car move slowly down the driveway.

"The car did not get stuck in the driveway," said Sebastian.

"No," said Nana. "The car did not get stuck in the driveway. You did a fine job of pushing the new snow away, Sebastian."

"Yes," said Sebastian. "I liked pushing the snow. When I grow up I'm going to be the chief snow pusher in the city."

"Good," said Nana. "Now come and have a cup of nice, hot cocoa."

Sebastian sang a little song as he went inside:

> "I'll shovel the bridges
> And sidewalks and streets,
> And then I'll come home
> For some nice Nana treats."

5. Sebastian Remembers a Promise

"I promised Jennifer that I'd find her Doolie Lamb," said Sebastian. "But I don't know where to look."

"We'll both look for Doolie Lamb in the morning," said Nana. "Finish your cocoa now and go to bed."

Sebastian went to bed. He was full of nice warm cocoa. The house was very quiet.
The wind was not whispering through the pine trees. Nobody was crying.

"This is a good time for me to remember where I put Doolie," thought Sebastian.
But Sebastian did not remember. Sebastian went to sleep.

After breakfast next day Sebastian began to hunt for Doolie.

"First I will look under the sofa," said Sebastian. Sebastian did not find Doolie Lamb under the sofa. He found a favourite tiny gold earring his mother had lost.

"Mom will be happy I found her favourite tiny gold earring," said Sebastian.

Sebastian looked for Doolie Lamb under a bunch of newspapers in the recycling box.

Sebastian did not find Doolie Lamb under the bunch of newspapers in the recycling box. He found a favourite screwdriver his father had lost.

"Dad will be happy I found his favourite screwdriver," said Sebastian.

Sebastian looked for Doolie Lamb in Nana's knitting basket. Sebastian did not find Doolie Lamb in Nana's knitting basket. He found a favourite red thimble his grandmother had lost.

"Nana! Nana! Look!" shouted Sebastian. "I have found your favourite red thimble. I have found Dad's favourite screwdriver. I have found Mom's favourite tiny gold earring!"

"That is just wonderful," said Nana. "Have you found Jennifer's Doolie Lamb?"

"Not yet," said Sebastian. "I will look for Doolie in my toy box. He must be there."

17

Sebastian dumped all the toys out of his toy box. Sebastian did not find Doolie.

He found a favourite dinosaur he had lost. It was a little orange brontosaurus.

"My orange brontosaurus!" said Sebastian. "It has been in my toy box all the time!"

"Did you find Jennifer's lamb?" asked Nana.

"I found my favourite little orange brontosaurus," said Sebastian, "but I did not find Doolie. Perhaps we can find another little white woolly lamb for Jennifer. We can call all the toy stores in town. When I visit Jennifer in the hospital tomorrow I will have a new little white lamb for her."

6. Sebastian Looks for a Look-Alike

"Do you have small white woolly lambs?" said Sebastian into the telephone.

"We have many, many small white lambs," said the lady in the first toy store, "but they are all made of plastic."

"Oh," said Sebastian. "Thank you, but they won't do."

"Do you have any small white woolly lambs?" said Sebastian into the telephone.

"We have many, many small woolly lambs," said the man in the second toy store, "but they are all black."

"Oh," said Sebastian. "Thank you, but they won't do.".

"Do you have any small white woolly lambs?" said Sebastian into the telephone.

"We have many, many soft woolly lambs," said the man in the third toy store, "but they are all very big."

"Oh," said Sebastian. "Thank you but they won't do."

20

Sebastian and Nana phoned all the toy stores in the city. Not one of them had a little soft white woolly lamb like Doolie.

"I will have to bring Jennifer something else when I visit her in the hospital this afternoon," said Sebastian. "She will be very disappointed."

"You did your best, Sebastian," said Nana.

"Yes, I did," said Sebastian. "But I broke my promise to Jennifer. I did not find Jennifer's Doolie Lamb and I did not find another one like it. Do you think Jennifer might like my little orange brontosaurus, Nana?"

"She might," said Nana.

7. Sebastian Wanders the Wards

Sebastian and Mom and Dad got on the hospital elevator. The elevator was full of people.

"Let me press the elevator button," said Sebastian. "What floor is Jennifer on?"

"Jennifer is on the fourth floor," said Dad. Sebastian pressed the '4' button. The elevator started going up. The elevator stopped. Some of the people got off the elevator.

"Do we get off here?" asked Sebastian

"No," said Mom. "We are only at the second floor."

The elevator started going up again. The elevator stopped. Some of the people got off the elevator.

"Do we get off here?" asked Sebastian.

"No," said Dad. "We are only at the third floor."

The elevator started going up again. The elevator stopped.

"This is where we get off," said Dad.

Sebastian and Dad and Mom walked down a long, long hall. There were doors on each side of the long hall.

"Which room is Jennifer in?" asked Sebastian.

"Jennifer is in a big room at the end of the hall," said Mom. "She is in a room with many other children. The big room is called a ward."

"Do all the other children in Jennifer's ward have hurting ears?" asked Sebastian.

"No," said Dad. "They each have different things wrong with them."

"Do I have to be very quiet?" asked Sebastian. "Like I do when Nana has a bad headache?"

"You have to be rather quiet," said Dad.

Sebastian looked in the door of the ward. He could not see Jennifer.

"I do not see Jennifer," said Sebastian.

"Jennifer is in the high bed by the window," said Mom. "She is looking out the window."

24

"Why does she have a big white bandage around her head?" asked Sebastian.

"Because the doctor had to make a small cut behind Jennifer's ear," said Dad. "The bandage is to keep the cut clean."

"Hi, Jennifer," said Sebastian.

Jennifer turned her head.

"Hi, 'Bastian," said Jennifer. "Did you bring me my Doolie Lamb?" Jennifer reached out her hand.

"I'm very sorry, Jennifer," said Sebastian. "I tried and tried, but I could not find Doolie."

"But you promised, 'Bastian, you promised," and Jennifer began to cry.

"Please don't cry, Jennifer," said Sebastian. "I could not bring you your Doolie Lamb, but I did bring you my little orange brontosaurus."

Sebastian put his little orange brontosaurus into Jennifer's hand.

Jennifer looked up at Sebastian and frowned a big frown. Jennifer looked down at the little orange brontosaurus and frowned a big frown.

"I don't want your little orange brontosaurus," sobbed Jennifer. "I want my Doolie Lamb."

Jennifer put her arm back and threw the little orange brontosaurus right across the room.

The little orange brontosaurus bounced on the floor and slid under a bed.

Sebastian crawled under the bed and picked up his little orange brontosaurus. He felt so sad that Jennifer was mad at him.

"I'll wait for you out in the hall, Mom and Dad," said Sebastian. "Goodbye Jennifer."

Sebastian waved to Jennifer. Jennifer did not wave to Sebastian.

Sebastian looked in the room next to Jennifer's ward. It was full of toys and books. It had a television set in one corner and a VCR. It had a whole shelf of videos beside the VCR.

"This hospital is not such a bad place to be," Sebastian said to a little boy who was watching *Theodore the Tugboat*.

"It is a very good place to get better," said the little boy. "And when you are almost all better, like I am, it is a great place."

"Do you know my sister Jennifer?" asked Sebastian.

"Is she the little girl in the bed by the window?" asked the little boy.

"Yes she is," said Sebastian.

"Yes," said the little boy. "I know Jennifer. She cries a lot."

"Oh dear," said Sebastian.

Sebastian went out into the hall again. He saw a smiling young woman pushing a cart with all sorts of little cartons on it.

"What's in those little cartons?" asked Sebastian.

"Ice cream," said the smiling young woman. "Would you like one?"

"Of course I would," said Sebastian. "Is there a chocolate one?"

"Yes," said the smiling young woman. She handed a chocolate one to Sebastian.

"Do you know my sister Jennifer?" asked Sebastian.

28

"Yes I do," said the smiling young woman. "Jennifer cries all the time."

"Oh dear, oh dear," said Sebastian as he sat down to eat his chocolate ice cream.

8. Sebastian Builds a Giant

"Nana," said Sebastian, "I am going to build a snowman right under Jennifer's window. It will be a huge snowman. It will be a wonderful surprise for Jennifer when she gets home this afternoon."

"It will be hard for you to build a huge snowman all by yourself, Sebastian," said Nana.

30

"Why don't you ask Mary Ann, your sitter from next door, to help?"

Mary Ann came to help Sebastian build a huge snowman right under Jennifer's window. Mary Ann brought her big black dog with her. Her big black dog's name was Friendly. Friendly dashed here and there around the yard.

Sebastian and Mary Ann rolled a huge ball of snow for the snowman's bottom half. Friendly raced back and forth across the yard.

Sebastian and Mary Ann rolled a middle-sized ball of snow for the snowman's top half. It was hard to lift up the middle-sized ball of snow. Friendly ran round and round and round the yard.

Sebastian and Mary Ann rolled the snowman's head.

"We need a stepladder to put the snowman's head on," said Sebastian.

31

"I'll get my dad's stepladder," said Mary Ann.

Sebastian climbed up the ladder. Friendly dashed here and there.

Sebastian reached down for the snowman's head. Friendly ran back and forth.

Sebastian lifted up the snowman's head. Friendly raced round and round and round.

Sebastian leaned over to put the snowman's head on. Friendly jumped up and down and crashed right into the ladder.

Up went the snowman's head. Over went the ladder.

Down went Sebastian into the deep, wet snow.

Over went the snowman on top of Sebastian.

"Yikes!" said Mary Ann. "We'll have to start again."

"Yes," said Sebastian, "but we will have to do it without Friendly's help."

32

"I will tie up Friendly," said Mary Ann.

"While you tie up Friendly I'll change my clothes. These clothes are very, very wet."

Sebastian went inside. He put on dry clothes.

"Nana," said Sebastian, "the snowman needs a hat."

"You can use your great-great grandfather's tall silk hat. It is in the attic."

"Thank you, Nana," said Sebastian.

"Nana," said Sebastian, "The snowman needs a scarf."

"You can use the long red scarf I have just finished knitting," said Nana.

"Thank you, Nana," said Sebastian.

Sebastian climbed the ladder. He put his great-great grandfather's tall silk hat on the snowman's head.

"That looks great!" said Mary Ann.

Mary Ann put two black corks, and a long orange carrot in the snowman's face for his eyes and his nose.

"That looks great!" said Sebastian.

Sebastian tied the long red scarf Nana had just finished knitting around the snowman's neck. Sebastian's dry clothes got all wet.

"That looks great!" said Mary Ann.

"That's the biggest and best snowman I have ever seen," said Nana.

"It's huge!" said Nancy.

"It's a giant," said Sebastian. "I hope Jennifer likes it!"

9. Sebastian is Held Up

"Your clothes are very, very wet, Sebastian," said Nana. "We will go to the basement and put both sets of wet clothes in the dryer."

"Let me," said Sebastian. Sebastian put his two sets of very, very wet clothes in the dryer. Nana showed Sebastian how to turn the dryer on warm for an hour.

"We must be careful," said Nana. "Sometimes this dryer doesn't turn off when it should."

"Get ready now, Sebastian," said Nana. "When you've had your bath, get dressed and come down for lunch. We will be leaving to get Jennifer from the hospital in an hour."

"Here is your Dad's car, Sebastian," said Nana. "Run down and make sure the dryer has stopped turning."

Sebastian ran down into the basement. The dryer had stopped turning. Sebastian opened the dryer. His two sets of very, very wet clothes were still a little wet. "I'll just put the dryer on again for another hour," said Sebastian.

"Hurry, Sebastian," Nana called. "We're waiting."

As Dad drove to the hospital Sebastian said, "I hope Jennifer will be ready."

Jennifer was ready.

On the way home Dad stopped the car. "Why have we stopped?" asked Sebastian.

"There must have been an accident on the bridge," said Dad.

"Oh dear," said Mom. "The doctor said Jennifer should be home in bed as soon as possible.

"I want to get home," cried Jennifer. "I want to see the surprise 'Bastian has for me."

"I brought you a peppermint, Jennifer," said Nana. "Would you like a peppermint too, Sebastian?" said Nana.

"Of course I would," said Sebastian. "We have been in the car a long time," said Sebastian.

"Yes," said Mom. "But we are starting to move now."

"Hurry, hurry," said Jennifer. "I want to see 'Bastian's surprise."

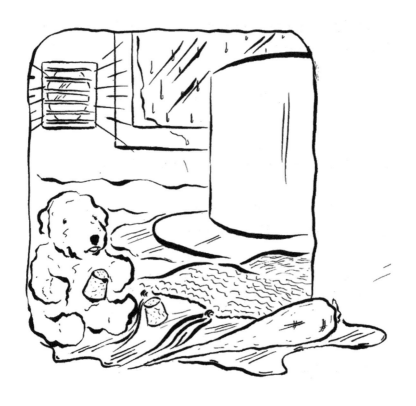

10. Sebastian Keeps his Word

"Oh 'Bastian," shouted Jennifer. Jennifer turned from her window and gave Sebastian a great, big hug. "You kept your promise!"

"I did?" said Sebastian. Sebastian looked out Jennifer's window.

Sebastian got a great surprise. He did not see a giant snowman.

Sebastian saw a large spot of green grass.

Sebastian saw his great-great grandfather's tall silk hat on the green grass.

Sebastian saw the new red scarf Nana had knitted on the green grass.

Sebastian saw two black corks and a carrot on the green grass.

Sebastian saw something else on the green grass. It was small and white and looked very, very wet.

"Why is Doolie down there?" wondered Sebastian. "And what has happened to my giant snowman?"

"You kept your promise, 'Bastian," said Jennifer. "You found my Doolie Lamb." And Jennifer hugged Sebastian again and again.

"Will you bring my Doolie Lamb up for me, 'Bastian?" asked Jennifer.

"Of course I will," said Sebastian.

Sebastian bent down to pick up Doolie. He felt something hot blowing on his face. The hot was coming from the house.

"Oh gosh!" said Sebastian. "The dryer! It's still on and that's what has melted my giant snowman."

Sebastian went down to the basement and turned off the dryer. He opened the dryer door and felt his clothes. They were very, very hot.

"Oh well," thought Sebastian as he climbed up the stairs to give Jennifer her precious lamb. At least I did find Doolie."

Sebastian sang a little song as he went upstairs:

> "My promise is kept,
> Because Doolie's okay,
> But I'm sorry my snowman
> Just melted away."

The End

About the Author

Gwen Molnar of Edmonton is a prize winning poet and prolific writer of children's poetry and stories. Her children's poetry has been dramatized on radio, television and in film.

Gwen has painted professionally for more than thirty years. In 1995, she won first prize in the Canadian Author's Association Poetry Contest for *"Around the World for a Shortcut."*

Her books include, *I Said to Sam* (Scholastic 1987) and *Animal Rap and Far-Out Stories* (Beach Holme, 1996), shortlisted for the 1997 Alberta Book Awards, Writer's Guild of Alberta. This is her second Hodgepog.

43

About the Illustrator

Kendra McClesky received her BA from Mount Holyoke College and studied fine art at the School of the Museum of Fine Arts in Boston, Massachusetts. She lives in Toronto with her husband, Ian, and two daughters, Merron and Haley. She is currently pursuing an MFA at the Ontario College of Art. She previously illustrated *Summer with Sebastian* (Hodgepog Books, 1997).

If you liked this book...
you might enjoy these other Hodgepog Books:

Read them yourself in grades 4-5, or read them to younger kids.

Ben and the Carrot Predicament
by Mar'ce Merrell, illustrated by Barbara Hartmann
ISBN 1-895836-54-9   Price $4.95

Getting Rid of Mr. Ribitus
by Alison Lohans, illustrated by Barbara Hartmann
ISBN 1-895836-53-0   Price $5.95

A Real Farm Girl
by Susan Ioannou, illustrated by James Rozak
ISBN 1-895836-52-2   Price $6.95

A Gift for Johnny Know-It-All
by Mary Woodbury, illustrated by Barbara Hartmann
ISBN 1-895836-27-1   Price $5.95

Mill Creek Kids
by Colleen Heffernan, illustrated by Sonja Zacharias
ISBN 1-895836-40-9   Price $5.95

Arly and Spike
by Luanne Armstrong, illustrated by Chao Yu
ISBN 1-895836-37-9   Price $4.95

A Friend for Mr. Granville
by Gillian Richardson, illustrated by Claudette MacLean
ISBN 1-895836-38-7   Price $5.95

Maggie and Shine
by Luanne Armstrong, illustrated by Dorothy Woodend
ISBN 1-895836-67-0   Price $6.95

Lost in a Blizzard
Constance Horne, Illustrated by Lori McGregor McCrae
ISBN 1-895836-69-7   Price $5.95

Butterfly Gardens
by Judith Benson, Illustrated by Lori McGregor McCrae
ISBN 1-895836-71-9   Price $5.95

---

and for readers in grades 1-2, or to read to pre-schoolers

Summer With Sebastian
by Gwen Molnar, illustrated by Kendra McCleskey
ISBN 1-895836-39-5   Price $4.95

The Noise in Grandma's Attic
by Judith Benson, illustrated by Shane Hill
ISBN 1-895836-55-7   Price $4.95